my first
Christmas
Bedtime
storybook

Disney PRESS
Los Angeles • New York

First Hardcover Edition, September 2020 10 9 8 7 6 5 4 3 2 1
ISBN 978-1-368-05270-2

FAC-025393-20164

Library of Congress Control Number: 2019910018
Printed in China

For more Disney Press fun, visit www.disneybooks.com

Contents

This book belongs to:

DISNEY

101 DALMATIANS

The Puppies' First Christmas

One winter evening, Pongo and Perdita were with their puppies when a rustling noise caught their attention. They all turned as Roger and Nanny hauled a HUGE TREE into the parlor.

"What's going on?" Rolly asked.

"DON'T WORRY, DEAR," said Perdita.

The parlor floor was covered in pine needles, boxes of ornaments, tinsel garlands, and strings of small lights. The puppies looked on as their human pets began acting VERY STRANGELY.

When the tree was finished, the lights and shiny ornaments cast a magical glow about the room.

That night, when Pongo and Perdita tucked the puppies into their basket, THEY TOLD THEM ALL ABOUT CHRISTMAS.

"It's a time when people show their families and friends how much they care for them," Pongo said.

Perdita continued. "On Christmas Eve people put presents under the tree to show their love."

"Christmas is about giving," Pongo told the puppies.

"I WONDER IF WE WILL GET ANY PRESENTS," said Rolly.

"I hope someone loves us," said Pepper.

"You are all loved whether or not there are presents under the tree," Perdita said. "Now time for bed. Tomorrow is a big day."

On Christmas morning, the puppies woke at dawn. They crept into the parlor. Sure enough, there were piles of brightly wrapped packages under the tree.

"WE ARE LOVED!" Pepper cried.

The puppies dove into the pile of presents. They tossed the packages around and ripped and tore at the colored paper.

Lucky pulled open a box. "Perfume?" he said, and wrinkled his nose.

Penny dragged a spotted necktie out of some tissue paper.

Just then they heard Roger and Anita's voices in the hallway.

"LET'S GET OUT OF HERE!" Rolly said.

The puppies hid and trembled when they heard Roger's footsteps. He stopped in the doorway, surprised.

The puppies looked at each other uncertainly.

Anita started to laugh.

Roger chuckled, too, and said, "Looks like we had some help opening our gifts." Then, with a twinkle in his eye, he called, "Here, pups!"

"There are still so many boxes to unwrap," Anita said. "I DO WISH THEY'D COME HELP."

One by one, the puppies crept from their hiding spots. They gathered around the tree as Roger pulled out more packages. "Go for it, boys and girls!"

The puppies tore into the bright wrappings and the tangled ribbons.

When the puppies grew tired of rolling around in the wrapping paper, Anita brought out a large basket.

She handed each puppy a squeaky toy.

"We like Christmas!" Pepper said.

"But remember what we told you about Christmas?" Perdita asked. "It's a time for giving."

"It's also about forgiving," Pongo said. "You were lucky that Roger and Anita weren't upset you unwrapped their presents."

The puppies' heads drooped a little. "WE'RE LUCKY WE HAVE TWO WONDERFUL HUMANS," Perdita said.

"WE ARE LOVED," Penny said. She smiled.

"You are all, each and every one of you, loved," Perdita assured her children.

"AND THAT'S WHAT CHRISTMAS IS REALLY ALL ABOUT," Pongo said as the puppies drifted off to sleep.

Ariel and Prince Eric were walking along the beach a few days before Christmas. Suddenly, Eric's dog, Max, ran up to them carrying a waterlogged boot.

This reminded Ariel, Eric needed a new pair of boots. She knew what to give him for Christmas!

Ariel and Eric returned to the castle. Carlotta, the housekeeper, announced it was time for tea.

"Already?" asked Grimsby, the butler, checking his pocket watch. "It must be broken."

Ariel remarked about the beauty of the tree and the red and gold decorations.

"THOSE ARE MY FAVORITE COLORS,"

Carlotta said. Now Ariel had gift ideas.

The next day, Ariel went into town to do her Christmas shopping. There she found boots for Eric, a shiny pocket watch for Grimsby, and a gold necklace with a ruby pendant for Carlotta. Then she got the biggest bone she could find for Max.

Ariel still needed gifts for her father and sisters. When she saw a shop window filled with glass hearts, she knew her search was over.

Back at the castle, Ariel carefully wrapped the gifts. She realized something was missing: it was Max's gift. Ariel heard a loud chewing noise coming from behind a chair.

Max was gnawing already on the bone she had gotten for him!

On Christmas morning, Ariel went to get everyone's gifts. But when she looked under her bed, all the gifts were gone!

She looked under the rug. Then she checked inside the closet.

BUT THE GIFTS WERE NOWHERE TO BE FOUND.

"Ariel!" Eric called upstairs. "It's time for presents!"

Ariel joined the prince by the tree. "Is it all right if we do this later? I promised my merfamily I would meet them at the beach." Ariel decided she could keep looking for the presents when she got back.

Ariel's friends were waiting on the beach. Scuttle the seagull handed Ariel a small chest.

Ariel lifted the lid and saw the sorts of treasures she had loved to collect when she was a mermaid. "Thank you!"

Just then, King Triton and Ariel's sisters swam up.

"MERRY CHRISTMAS!" Ariel said.

"We brought presents!" Ariel's sister Aquata shouted.

"Oh, thank you!" Ariel exclaimed. "I have gifts for all of you, too, except—"

Max ran up, holding a boot, and Eric had arrived.

"Your present!" Ariel said to Eric. Now she knew where the missing gifts were. Max had buried them on the beach!

"Surprise, everyone! We're going on a Christmas-gift treasure hunt!" Soon Eric, Carlotta, Max, and Grimsby were digging around on the beach.

Ariel's friends and merfamily cheered them on.

EVERYONE LOVED ARIEL'S GIFTS.

After the treasure hunt was over, they gathered by the water's edge to say good-bye.

"MERRY CHRISTMAS!" they called to each other as Ariel and Eric headed back to the castle.

The Sweetest Christmas

One snowy Christmas Eve, Winnie the Pooh had set up a tree in his living room. It was decorated with some candles in honey pots. Pooh looked at the tree and tapped his head.

"SOMETHING SEEMS TO BE MISSING," he said.

Suddenly, a knock startled Pooh. When Pooh opened the door, he found a small snowman on his front step.

"H-h-he-l-l-l-o, P-Pooh B-Bear," the snowman said. His voice sounded very familiar. Pooh invited the snowman inside.

After standing by the fire, the snowman began to melt. HE STARTED TO LOOK LIKE PIGLET!

Piglet saw Pooh's glowing Christmas tree.

"Are you going to string popcorn for your tree?" Piglet asked.

"There was popcorn and string," Pooh said. "But now there is only string." Pooh wondered if popcorn was what he'd forgotten. But that wasn't it.

"Then we can use the string to wrap the presents you're giving," Piglet said.

"I forgot to get presents!" Pooh exclaimed. Soon it was time for Piglet to leave. Pooh stood beside his tree and thought about the presents he forgot.

THEN HE
HAD AN IDEA.

He still didn't know what to do about the presents, but he knew where to find help.

"Hello!" Pooh called as he knocked on Christopher Robin's door.

"Come in, Pooh Bear!" Christopher Robin said. "Merry Christmas! Why do you look so sad?"

"Christopher Robin," Pooh said, "what if someone forgot to find presents for his friends?"

Christopher Robin gave Pooh stockings for each of his friends. "You can put their gifts in here," he said.

Pooh hurried off to deliver the stockings to his friends.

As he walked through the Hundred-Acre Wood, he thought about the presents he still needed for the stockings.

Pooh stopped at each friend's house. He quietly hung the stockings where his friends would find them. Each one had a tag that read *From Pooh*.

When Pooh got back to his house, he climbed into his cozy chair. "Now I must think of presents for my friends," he said. Before he knew it, HE WAS FAST ASLEEP.

The next morning, Pooh awoke to a loud thumping noise. He climbed out of the chair and opened the door.

"Merry Christmas, Pooh!" his friends cried.

All his friends were carrying the stockings from Pooh. Pooh realized he had fallen asleep before giving presents to his friends. Then Pooh realized they were all thanking him for their gifts!

"No more cold ears in the winter with my new cap," Piglet said.

All Pooh's friends had found the stockings quite useful.

Pooh looked at his friends. They were very happy with their stockings, even though there weren't any presents in them!

"SOMETHING VERY NICE IS GOING ON,"
Pooh said.

"It is very nice, Pooh Bear," Piglet said.

"It's called Christmas, buddy bear," Tigger said. He patted Pooh on the back.

Pooh watched in surprise as each of his friends presented him with a honey pot.

"I don't know what to say," Pooh told his friends. He was thrilled by their gifts. Honey was his favorite treat!

"CHRISTMAS IS A WONDERFUL HOLIDAY," Rabbit said. "Especially when you have good friends to share it with."

"Yep!" Tigger agreed. "But I know how we could make the day even sweeter."

He looked at the honey pot in Pooh's hands. An idea tickled at Pooh's brain.

"Let's all have lunch together!" Pooh said. He passed out the honey pots his friends had just given him.

Minnie Saves Christmas

Mickey, Minnie, and their friends had been working hard preparing for Christmas—and it was only ONE DAY AWAY!

Suddenly, a timer rang. Minnie jumped up. "My cookies are ready! Who wants one?"

As Minnie took the cookies out of the oven, there was a loud crash in the other room! Goofy dove under the table. "Gawrsh! What was that?"

Minnie looked toward the living room. "It sounded like it came from the fireplace."

Donald looked excited. "MAYBE IT'S SANTA CLAUS!"

Everyone raced to the fireplace. But it wasn't Santa Claus. . . . It was MRS. CLAUS! "Merry Christmas, everyone!"

Minnie was surprised. "Why, Mrs. Claus, what brings you here?"

Mrs. Claus looked at her friends. "OH, I NEED YOUR HELP! Santa accidentally shrunk his mittens and his big red bag when he ran them through the wash. And now I'm afraid he won't be able to deliver presents tonight!"

Donald was shocked. "What? No presents?"

Goofy shook his head. "I wish we had an
UNSHRINKING MACHINE!"

Minnie thought for a moment and then made a
dash for the kitchen. "I know just what we need!"

Minutes later, Minnie returned. "Santa could use this big red tablecloth for a bag!" Minnie said. "And we can tie it shut with this ribbon. And he can wear these oven mitts as mittens!"

Mickey smiled. "Great idea, Minnie!"

Mrs. Claus beamed. "Oh, thank you, Minnie!
YOU SAVED CHRISTMAS!"

Minnie giggled. "It was my pleasure!"

"Well, I'd better hurry back to the North Pole.
Who wants to come with me?"

Everyone cheered as they climbed into the sleigh
with Mrs. Claus and took off into the sky.

Santa was waiting for them when they arrived
at the North Pole. "Thank goodness you're back—
and just in the nick of time, too!" Everyone pitched
in to help the elves load Santa's sleigh.

Just then, Pluto started barking. He wanted to help, too! Minnie used the rest of her ribbon to make a special harness for Pluto—with an extra-special bow, of course!

Mrs. Claus, Minnie, and the rest of the gang waved as the reindeer—and Pluto—pulled Santa's sleigh up, up, up into the night sky. It was going to be THE BEST CHRISTMAS EVER!

Disney
Sleeping Beauty

Aurora's Homemade Holiday

One snowy December day, Princess Aurora and Prince Phillip went for a stroll. As they walked, Phillip noticed the princess was unusually quiet. "Is something the matter?" he asked.

"My aunts and I used to love Christmastime," she said. The three fairies Flora, Fauna, and Merryweather had raised Aurora.

"Let's invite them for the holidays," Phillip said.

The next morning Prince Phillip sent an invitation to Flora, Fauna, and Merryweather before he and Samson left for a trip.

Soon the good fairies arrived. Princess Aurora had a special request for them.

"You want Christmas *exactly* like the ones we shared at the cottage?" Flora asked. "THAT MEANS WE CAN'T USE MAGIC."

"You'd better take our wands," Fauna said to Aurora. But the wands were hard to catch.

"SHALL WE DECORATE?" Aurora asked. She led the fairies to baskets of evergreen garlands, ornaments, and bows.

Aurora suggested that she and Flora put up the evergreen garlands while Fauna and Merryweather decorated the Christmas tree.

After a busy morning, the last stocking was finally hung above the fireplace. Then Aurora and the fairies moved on to the kitchen. It was time to begin baking their Christmas treats.

"I can't wait until Phillip tastes your special layer cake," Aurora said, "and the rolls with jam inside."

The next morning over breakfast, Aurora and the good fairies talked about a gift for Phillip.

"I want to give him a homemade present," Aurora said, "but what?"

"How about a shirt?" Flora suggested.

"But I don't know how to sew," the princess replied.

"WE'LL SHOW YOU HOW," Merryweather said.

The fairies were excited to teach Aurora all about planning a homemade holiday gift.

All morning, the fairies worked with Aurora, teaching her how to cut fabric and how to sew a shirt.

"Oh, dear," the princess said when she looked down at her sewing. "THIS SHIRT ISN'T LOOKING QUITE RIGHT."

The fairies quickly set aside their own projects to help Aurora with Phillip's shirt.

When Aurora finished Phillip's gift, the fairies helped her get ready. The prince would be home soon.

The fairies made a crown of holly for the princess's hair. Next they had to decide what she would wear. Flora suggested a red dress. Merryweather preferred a blue one. Then Fauna held up a beautiful purple gown. Aurora tried it on. The dress was perfect!

The last thing Aurora had to do was wrap the prince's gift. Once again, SHE ASKED FOR THE FAIRIES' HELP. When they were finished, the princess placed the present under the tree.

That afternoon, Prince Phillip arrived back at the castle.

"Close your eyes," the princess said with a sly grin, "and don't open them until I tell you to."

Aurora led Phillip into the grand hall, where Flora, Fauna, and Merryweather were waiting.

"Okay ... NOW OPEN YOUR EYES!" Aurora exclaimed.

Phillip looked around.

"I've never seen preparations like these before," he said.

"Try a lemon tart," Aurora said.

Phillip took one and bit into it. Suddenly, a strange look came over his face.

"Oh, dear," Fauna said, "we forgot the sugar!"

Aurora handed Phillip his gift. "ONE MORE SURPRISE!" she said.

"A shirt!" the prince exclaimed after opening the box.

"Oh, dear, that's certainly not the right size," Aurora said.

"No," said Phillip, "but there's more here to love." Then he wrapped Aurora in a hug, so thankful for a homemade holiday.

The Best Present Ever

"**H**ey, Lightning—look at me!" Mater sledded past his best buddy, Lightning McQueen. CHRISTMAS WAS JUST A FEW DAYS AWAY. The two friends were taking turns sliding down a snow-covered hill using Mater's one-of-a-kind junkyard sled.

"I can't wait to take this sled to Kersploosh Mountain on Christmas!" Mater said. Kersploosh Mountain was a water park near Radiator Springs.

"Uh, Mater, remember that Russian Ice Racers Cup I told you I was competing in?"

"Well, sure," said Mater. "The one in a few weeks."

"That's just it, they moved it up to this week. I'm not going to be here for Christmas after all."

Lightning felt bad but told Mater they could do something else when he got back.

Mater pulled into Flo's V8 Café. He told Flo how Lightning wasn't going to be around for Christmas.

"That's too bad," Flo said. "I guess you'll have to celebrate early."

"That's a good idea!" Mater said. He suddenly realized he forgot presents. He had to get Lightning a present!

"Luigi!" Mater yelled as he skidded up to Casa Della Tires. **"I NEED YOUR HELP!"**

Luigi smiled. "For you, Mater, anything!"

"Those snow tires," said Mater. "The ones that used to be in the front window."

Luigi's smile faded. "Someone's already bought them. They just left a moment ago."

Outside a big truck with new snow tires was driving away from the shop.

Mater raced after the truck. "I need those tires for my best buddy's Christmas gift."

"Sorry," the truck replied, "but I've been dreaming of speeding through the snow with these superfast tires."

"I'll bet my sled is faster going down that hill than you in those tires. IF I'M RIGHT, WE'LL TRADE. Deal?" Mater said. The truck agreed, and Mater zipped down the hill, beating the truck.

Meanwhile, Sally helped Lightning decide that he didn't need to go to that race and could stay for Christmas with his best buddy.

Lightning couldn't wait to tell Mater the good news. On his way to see his best buddy, he drove past a sign for Kersploosh Mountain. HE HAD AN IDEA FOR THE PERFECT GIFT.

The next day, Lightning and Mater exchanged gifts. Lightning unwrapped the tires.

Lightning was touched. Mater was already ripping open his gift. When he saw the two tickets to Kersploosh Mountain, his eyes grew wide.

Lightning shrugged. "I decided not to go to my race, so now I can spend Christmas with you, buddy."

"Hey, where is your sled?" Lightning asked, looking around.

Mater shuffled nervously. "Uh, I may have traded it to get you them there SNOW TIRES."

A twinkle came to Lightning's eye. "Mater—didn't your old sled have bumper tires?"

On Christmas Day, Mater and Lightning sat at the top of Kersploosh Mountain. Beneath them was a new junkyard sled.

"It's Mater's Junkyard Sled 2.0, with double the sledding fun!" cried Mater.

"You ready for this?" Lightning asked.

"YOU BET," said Mater.